Laura has two beautiful children, on who the story is based. She has lived in the Cheshire countryside all her life and likes to spend time outdoors. She has an interest in wildlife, as do her young children and often spends time looking after animals.

The story was based on a true event, but in real life, the magpie was rescued and taken to a local animal hospital for injured wildlife. The magpie was nursed back to health and later released back into the wild.

Laura is a teacher and knew from an early age that she wanted to work with children. She has been a primary school teacher for 17 years. Latterly she focused her career more towards supporting children with additional needs and those that are cared for. She thoroughly enjoys her job and hopes her writing will inspire young writers of the future.

BLUEBELL COTTAGE MAGPIE MISHAP

LAURA HEMMING

AUSTIN MACAULEY PUBLISHERS™
LONDON • CAMBRIDGE • NEW YORK • SHARJAH

A CIP catalogue record for this title is available from the British Library.

ISBN 9781398459649 (Paperback)
ISBN 9781398459656 (ePub e-book)

www.austinmacauley.com

First Published 2023
Austin Macauley Publishers Ltd®
1 Canada Square
Canary Wharf
London
E14 5AA

My wonderful best friend – Suzanne, who has illustrated the book amazingly.

My fabulous friends and family who provide endless support.

The head teacher Mrs Fau-Goodwin and all the staff and inspirational children at St Marys RC School for believing in me.

Lower Moss Wood – animal hospital (where the animal was taken to).

My beautiful children – Noah and Ruby, who have helped me so much with the imaginative and magical ideas and continue to bring me happiness only a daily basis. Thank you for both being so wonderful. You are my absolute world.

♡

Chapter One
Fairy Greeting

Seth Speller from being very young had always been eager to learn about animals and was a member of the local nature society. He wanted to be a zoologist, and he loved spending his time reading animal encyclopaedias and watching animal documentaries. Although he was only eight, he was keen in saving the planet for future generations.

He and his sister would often pick up litter around their village to help protect the planet. His little sister, Maisy, also loved animals and her favourite was a flamingo, mainly because it was pink! Pink was Maisy's favourite colour and although like her brother she liked looking after the planet and being outside with nature, building dens and climbing trees, she also liked playing dress up and wearing her mummy's make up.

Their favourite day out was the zoo, as it was full of exotic animals. Seth especially liked visiting the big cats and he could watch the Sumatran tigers for hours, especially the young tiger cubs when they were playing in the pool on a hot summer's day.

Maisy loved visiting the flamingo enclosure; particularly since it had recently been altered, so that there was a special footbridge across the flamingo lake which meant visitors to the zoo could get much closer to the beautiful, flamboyant animals.

Although they both loved their day trips to the zoo, they really liked returning home to Bluebell cottage, as the children had a very special secret. They couldn't help any of the animals in the zoo, but the wild animals that lived near Bluebell cottage, they could...

Chapter Two
Fairy Life

Seth first realised there were fairies at the bottom of his garden when he was only three years old. He had been looking for bugs and uncovering them from rocks and upturned bark. It was underneath a red and white spotty toadstool that he found his first ever fairy. He was really shocked and at first thought he was dreaming. By the time he shouted for his mum to look, the fairy had quickly hidden. Seth continued exploring and on one occasion, he wrote a small note to them explaining he wasn't going to hurt them.

He met and spoke to his first fairy, however, when he was four and had left a tooth under his pillow. Seth had gone to bed like any other night. He always struggled to go to sleep, as he always had so many ideas and facts swimming around in his head.

It was a warm summer's evening, and he had his bedroom window open slightly, so he could hear the sound of the birds and geese flying over the cottage. He was just drifting off to sleep when he heard a small tapping sound; he sleepily looked up to his window to see a small fairy climbing through it. Seth spoke to the fairy, and the fairy jumped in shock and fell from the window sill. The fairy lay motionless on his bedroom floor. Seth carefully picked him up and gently rested him upon his soft pillow. When the fairy eventually woke up, Seth explained, just like his previous note had said that he wasn't going to hurt the fairy. To Seth's surprise, the fairy spoke back and to the astonishment of both Seth and the fairy they realised that they could understand each other.

The fairy also explained that they had received Seth's note, but they had never found a time to be able to see Seth on his own, because grown-ups were never to see the fairies, as they didn't believe in fairies.

The fairies believed the grown-ups would hurt them, but they knew that children believed in magic!

Seth later learnt that this fairy was the leader of all the fairies that lived within the village at the bottom of Seth's garden, and he was known as the Wise One. They went on to become great friends. Every time Seth lost a tooth, he knew he was going to have a visit from the Wise One, and it was around a year later that Seth was out in the garden bug hunting once again that he saw the toadstool village that the Wise One had talked about.

It fascinated Seth and he peered closer to have a look at the detail in the small, miniature village. The tables were made from small twigs and leaves, with acorn cups and bowls placed upon them. They had used everything from the environment to create their wonderful, magical village and what was so lovely, was that every single fairy looked happy and content.

Chapter Three
The Secret

Seth spent many summers watching the goings on in the small fairy village, and Seth and the Wise One would talk often about nature and looking after the planet. It was on a late summer afternoon that Seth was sat at the bottom of his garden playing when he saw a worm come out of the ground and one of the fairies talk to it. He couldn't believe his eyes or his ears for that matter. The worm explained to the fairy that he was feeling unwell and the fairy flew away to another toadstool and returned with an acorn cup filled with liquid. The worm squirmed away feeling much happier.

It so happened that Seth's younger sister had lost her first tooth that day and so Seth knew it was time to share his secret with Maisy.

That night Seth introduced the fairies to his sister, Maisy. Maisy was super excited and couldn't believe how beautiful and delicate the fairy's wings were. Seth also used the time to ask the Wise One about what he had seen earlier that day between the worm and the fairy in the fairy village. The Wise One was surprised as he didn't realise that humans couldn't communicate with animals. Seth suddenly realised how they could all help each other.

The special magic between them was that the fairies could communicate with the animals and the fairies could also talk to Seth and Maisy. This meant that they could tell the children what help the animals needed, and the children could help the fairies with the animals.

Over the following year, Seth and Maisy spent as much time as possible down at the bottom of the garden, watching the fairies live their everyday life. Maisy loved watching the female fairies as they had such beautiful dresses and delicately fragile wings. Maisy even gave some of her doll's dresses to them, and they were thrilled. They would use glow worm silk or spider cobweb to stitch and darn with.

Seth would watch them going about their everyday business, but on a smaller scale and would be fascinated by how much they used nature to live by. They had a small well in the centre of the fairy village, with which they collected rain water in acorn cups and pulled on ivy trails.

Their houses were made from leaves and twigs and they would have help from some garden ants to fetch and carry if they needed it.

The whole fairy village was always very busy, but everyone worked together as a team, and it was like watching a well-oiled machine working. All the fairies had come to accept Seth and his sister, Maisy, and actually were pleased to see them arrive. Both the children learnt a lot from them, especially gaining knowledge from the Wise One. Seth found it really hard to understand why, as human's, we didn't live more like them and why so much plastic and waste was produced.

Seth was really keen to look after the planet and was always on at his parents to do more to look after it. As a family they grew their own vegetables and tried to limit the packaging they used when shopping. Seth would also make posters to display around the village and promote people to look after the planet.

He got really excited on the day his monthly national geographic magazine arrived, as it always gave him more ideas on how to save the planet. He often wrote to companies asking them to consider their effect on the planet too. He appeared in the local newspaper once for his tree planting initiative.

Chapter Four
Magpie's Misery

Seth discovered he could truly help the wild animals following a very windy night. The tree branches scratching against his bedroom window had kept him awake most of the night, and in the morning, Seth and Maisy had rushed out to the garden even before breakfast to check on the fairies and their village. Thankfully the village was all intact.

The children returned to the house grateful that there was no real damage, but a few pieces of fallen brash from the tall pine tree that towered the back garden. They both settled at the breakfast bar and their mum poured their cereal out and got them their favourite milk from the local dairy farm.

Seth and Maisy then heard a noise at the cat flap, but could see both their cats snuggled on the sofa together. The fairies had learnt they could enter Bluebell cottage through the cat flap, if there were no open windows. It was risky, so they only did it if there was an injured animal. The children turned to see Lilac, a flower fairy, and Fern, the pixie.

The children ate their breakfast as fast as they could, asked to be excused by their parents and then ran upstairs to get dressed. They were in such a hurry. Maisy put her clothes over her princess pyjamas and Seth forgot to brush his teeth. They told their parents they were going to tidy the garden following the bad wind. They both pulled on their wellies and waterproof coats and ran outside.

Lilac and Fern met the children at the back door, and they had told them that a magpie nest had fallen out of the large pine tree in their back garden in the really high winds.

Seth had seen some pine brash on the ground, but hadn't realised that there was a hurt bird in there. There had been two magpie chicks, as the fairies had been checking on them. They had been doing really well, but had not been ready to leave the nest. In the high winds, the parents had flown off to get more shelter, but when the nest had fallen, the parents had not returned.

Unfortunately one of the chicks had not made it, but there was one (very noisy) magpie chick without its parents. Seth asked the fairies what he should do; they told him that the magpie was hungry and needed food, and that it was very scared. He asked the fairies to reassure the chick and to tell it that he and his sister were there to help.

Chapter Five
The Rescue

Seth made his way into the garden and using a cloth, he gently covered over the chick and picked it up and brought it back inside. Maisy found a strong cardboard box and called their mum to help. Seth told his mum that he thought the magpie chick was hungry; she quickly researched what to feed a magpie chick, so they made a paste of cat biscuits and warm water and fed the magpie with a medicine syringe, just like it's mum would have fed it food. The magpie chick clearly loved it and calmed really quickly.

Maisy decided to call the chick Matilda the magpie (Tilly for short) and both Seth and she took it in turns to mix the biscuits and water and feed the chick every few hours with the help of their mum or dad. They positioned the box in the utility room, where it was nice and warm from the tumble dryer, but so it was also safe from the two house cats. The chick sat on an old towel within the cardboard box, which they frequently changed as it messed a lot!

Days went by and the magpie gained strength and weight. Lilac and Fern checked in with the magpie each day. The magpie went from eating cat biscuits to worms and other insects, which the fairies helped Seth and Maisy collect. In the meantime, the magpie's parents returned and built another nest, but in the lower branches of the pine tree to make it more secure.

Chapter Six
The Flight

Fern and Lilac were able to tell the very relieved magpie parents that the chick was gaining strength and that the humans in Bluebell cottage were looking after her. The fairies gave daily reports to the magpie's parents, and the chick was delighted to hear that they had made another nest.

As the days passed, Tilly got stronger and stronger, until one day she was finally strong enough to be released back into the wild. Fern and Lilac explained to Tilly that she was strong enough and big enough now to be released, so she could join her mum and dad back in the tall pine tree in the back garden of Bluebell cottage. Seth and Maisy carefully carried the cardboard box outside and lay it on the picnic table.

Tilly flapped her wings, but nothing happened. She didn't fly upwards. She tried again, but still nothing. Everyone looked on in shock and couldn't believe that the little chick could not fly. Seth thought quickly and asked the fairies to show Tilly what to do, so they flew down on to the picnic bench alongside Tilly and demonstrated to her how to fly off. Tilly watched on in amazement and was determined to learn.

She could hear her parents in the nest within the tall pine tree and she was eager to fly to them. All afternoon, with the fairies help, she kept practising, until just as the sun was setting in the sky and the air was turning colder, she did it! Both Seth and Maisy were delighted. They let out a whoop and a cheer which startled Fern and Lilac, but soon everyone was laughing and happy that Tilly had made a full recovery and made it back to her parents in the nest.

Chapter Seven
Leaving the Nest

As the year continued to progress, so did Tilly. Seth and Maisy often sat in the garden looking up from the trampoline at the branches of the pine tree. They would often see Tilly and her parents flying to and from the nest. It was now difficult to tell Tilly and her parents apart, as she had grown so much and looked just like an adult bird now.

It was one crisp, autumn morning when the fairies came to speak to Seth and Maisy and explained that it was time for Tilly to leave the nest and fly away to find a new home.

Although both the children were disappointed, they understood that in nature, young animals leave their parents much younger than humans do, and Tilly had made a full recovery from her nasty fall, thanks to the kindness from the children, so it was only right that she move on.

Also this way, it meant she might find a partner, come next spring and hopefully she would have her own young ones to feed and protect.

So it was with a little sadness, but joy that Tilly was strong enough to move on. That afternoon, the children and the fairies gathered in the back garden of Bluebell cottage to wave a fond farewell to Tilly and wish her all best for the future.

She told the fairies to thank both Maisy and Seth for all their hard work in helping her get better, and she also told the fairies that she would come back and visit and hoped to bring her own family back one day to visit the tall pine tree in the garden of Bluebell cottage.

Everyone then stood and watched as Tilly flew from the nest and into the distance in the direction of the local lake which was surrounded by tall pine trees. Seth and Maisy were sorry to see her go, but pleased that they had achieved their first animal rescue together with the help of the fairies, and it wasn't long before the next animal needed their help...

THE END